THE ADVENTURES OF BEAU AND QUINCY

THE SULTAN AND THE SEA SHELL

BY
PAMELA CHARLSTON DE GROOD

The Adventures of Beau and Quincy

Published Second Edition
August 2023

Copyrights © 2023

All rights reserved

Dedication

This book is dedicated to my mother, Mary Ann Charlston. She is an incredible person, mother, and grandmother.

She taught me how to love dogs and how a dog can always be your best friend.

"... here are some words to get you by. To help you on the journey of your life. You'll need a good dog. Especially a good dog."

    Jake Owen
    The Journey of Your Life
    Barefoot Blue Jean Night

The Adventures of Beau and Quincy

Contents

Dedication iii

Chapter 1: The Shiny Shell 1

Chapter 2: Whoosh…Flash 7

Chapter 3: A Magical Landing 15

Chapter 4: Boy with the Flute 19

Chapter 5: A Royal Bath 27

Chapter 6: The Gift 33

Chapter 7: 1775 39

Chapter 8: No Computers 48

Chapter 9: Plan to Get Home 52

Chapter 10: Cowry Hunt 57

Chapter 11: The Market Crowd 61

Chapter 12: The Necklace 67

Chapter 13: The Marked Spot 74

Chapter 14: Home Sweet Home 78

Vocabulary 80

The Adventures of Beau and Quincy

Chapter 1:
The Shiny Shell

Beau and Quincy are Labrador Retrievers who live with their mother and father in Florida in the cold winter months and live up in the northeast parts of the United States in the hot summer months. They have a happy and very entertaining life and are well cared for by their owners. Beau and Quincy are well-behaved dogs. They fetch tennis balls on the beach, go on many walks with Mom and Dad and occasionally get into some trouble.

But, overall, they are, as Mom and Dad say, "perfect dogs."

One November morning, after a scrumptious kibbles breakfast and an under-the-table blueberry from Dad's bowl, the house in Florida was notoriously quiet. Mom was reading, and Dad was resting after the long and monotonous* car ride from New York City. It took two long days with many stops to stretch dog and people's legs and to use the absolute "all-animal necessities," which Mom and Dad were kind enough to never make Beau and Quincy wait too long!

One sleepover in a pet-friendly hotel was always on the agenda, too, as Dad despised to do the trip straight!

"That was a crazy-fun Thanksgiving with all our cousins in the city, wasn't it Quincy," exclaimed Quincy as he rolled over onto his back while wagging his tail at the same time.

"Oh yes," yawned Beau as he stretched his legs and toes and arched his back, "I just loved rolling around on the floor and fetching balls and toys and especially eating their candy and treats from the table! It was dog heaven! That youngest one, Charlotte, with the curls singing and even trying to ride us was a bit tough on my body." Stretching, he stood up and sighed, "I have to admit, my back does ache a bit."

"Well," said Quincy arching his own sore back from the car ride, "we have a while now till we get our first visitors here in Florida, so you can rest that back. Come on, let's go sniff out the house and see what we missed while we were up north."

"There seems to be a lot of changes," said Beau. "So many new colors and so many new pieces of furniture. Ooh, and so many new little baubles*, aaahhh," a strange sound came out of his mouth as he stretched his neck up as high as he could like a giraffe. "I can't seem to reach any of the cool ones. Hmm, I think I can grab that shiny giant shell! It looks much different than the ones that we find on the beach here."

Beau scanned all around him and made sure that Mom and Dad were not coming before he reached for the shell.

"Aaa hah, got it!"

The shell almost hit the floor as Beau grabbed onto it with a soft clench of his teeth so he wouldn't break it. He knew that if he broke it, Mom would be very sad. Mom loved to collect valuable antiques from her travels.

"Careful," said Quincy, "Mom will hear." Quincy knew that Mom was a light napper, but Dad would sleep through anything!

Chapter 2:
Whoosh...Flash

"I got it. Come on! Hide in under the couch pillow now! I hear someone coming," Beau whispered.

Both dogs suddenly lay looking innocently lazy and sleepy in their spots on the floor.

"It's a good thing," Quincy whispered, "that dogs have their own language!"

"Hi Boys," said Dad as he gave them a good rub on their bellies. "You look so exhausted laying there. Yeah...it was a long trip yesterday. Today we'll rest, boys and your mom and I will go out to a party tonight. Before we go, though, we'll take you for one of your favorite walks on the beach. See ya later, boys. I'm heading to golf."

"Phew, that was close," said Beau. "Let's leave the shell hidden and go find Mom in the kitchen.

I hear her. She is up already. She must be looking at her computer and tapping buttons. I thought she would rest longer. Maybe she's looking at those pictures from all of her amazing adventures. Let's go see."

The two dogs stretched their bodies, yawned and lazily pattered into the kitchen.

"Hey, Beau and Quincy," said Mom as she patted Beau and Quincy on the heads and backs. "I'm just looking at pictures from our trip in November. We went with Margie and Skip. You remember them. Look boys…the beaches were spectacular with such white sand. This place is called the Maldives. The island we stayed on was called Atolls. We went on some fabulous adventures while we were there. Look closely, and I'll show you all of the pictures on the computer screen." Mom turned the computer so the dogs could see and began clicking through each picture. "Look at the blue crystal clear water, boys. You would have loved to just jump in!"

While gazing at the pictures, Beau thought to himself how much he would love to explore those white sandy beaches. He began to imagine the smells of the ocean and the feeling of the crisp salt water on his feet.

Quincy, on the other hand, began picturing himself running down the white sandy beach, throwing the sand to and fro and then digging a big hole to see if he could find a treasure. He imagined chasing the waves and finding an excellent piece of driftwood to toss around and an old rotten smelly fish.

Beau and Quincy stared at the picture of the beach frozen on the computer screen while Mom got up to answer the phone in the office. All of a sudden, Quincy noticed the shell that they had stolen earlier off the table. The same shell that they had hidden under the couch pillow. There it was, just lying on the sand in the picture on the computer screen. The same exact one!

Quincy said to Beau, "Look, there it is!"

An actual dog bark escaped his mouth as he was so excited.

Quincy ran to get the shell from under the pillow on the couch to confirm that it was the same one. He stood in front of the computer with it in his mouth.

"Wow," Beau said, "You are right, that's the exact one from the picture! I guess Mom brought it home!"

Beau and Quincy held the shell together carefully and stared at the screen.

In the next moment, both Beau and Quincy felt like they were spinning in circles. They were overcome with a dizzy and weak feeling as they continued to stare at the beach picture on the computer screen. All at once the picture became blurry. They both squeezed their eyes shut while holding the shell. They opened their eyes again and suddenly the air became very hot until a flash of wind hit them and spun them around, making their fur stand up on end like electricity was traveling through them.

Beau and Quincy were breathing so fast they could barely catch their breath! Whoosh... they felt their paws come off the kitchen floor as they were lifted into the air. They were scared but could still see the computer screen, but now the picture became bigger and bigger and the beach became bigger and bigger and it looked and felt like they were flying and looking down at the beach.

Flash...a bright light surrounded them and then just as suddenly, everything went black.

Chapter 3:
A Magical Landing

As quickly as all went black, the world became light again. The electricity feeling was now gone, but the warm air was still surrounding Beau and Quincy.

"Wow," Beau exclaimed. "What happened? Where are we?"

Wiggling his toes and squishing his feet into the ground, and realized that they were standing on sand.

"Can you believe it?" Quincy yelled out! "This is the whitest sand I have ever seen in my life! It feels funny."

He began to roll over and over in it until he realized that the sand was sticking to every hair on his body and that the sand was prickly.

"Actually, this is not so good." He began to shake vigorously to get the sand off him. He cried, "I think it is stuck to me forever!"

"Quincy!" Beau barked, raising his dog voice at his brother, "Enough about the *sssssand*. Do you realize what has just happened to us? We were just *sssssucked* into the computer, into one of Mom's pictures! We're doomed!"

Quincy then sat up, finished shaking off the sand and sat down next to Beau. The two dogs were sitting on the most beautiful white sandy beach surrounded by the calmest, bluest water that they had ever seen. Everything around them was quiet and warm.

They could hear the ever-so-slight sound of music in the distance that seemed to travel with the light breeze that was blowing down the beach. The peace, beauty, and serenity overwhelmed the two dogs. They lay down exhausted.

They both crossed their paws and rested their heads on them. They stared into the distant blue sparkling water with Mom's shell beside them and dozed off.

Quincy and Beau were excited, confused, and overwhelmed.

Their transport through the computer and the beauty were all so magical.

Chapter 4:
Boy with the Flute

While Beau and Quincy lay sleeping, a regal-looking* young boy happened upon them and immediately dropped his flute on Quincy's head in surprise. In all of his 11 years, he had never seen any animals such as these dogs, so he was petrified; as Quincy began to wake up, the boy was terrified that he would end up as these fearsome creatures 'dinner.

Quincy rolled over and stretched his long, strong, and muscular body with a big yawn until he suddenly remembered where he was.

Then he bolted upright and immediately tripped and fell on top of his brother. Beau then slowly opened one big brown eye and sighed at his younger brother's antics*. Then he saw the scared-looking young boy standing over them.

They both stared directly at the boy.

"Who is that?" Beau asked.

"I have no idea." said Quincy, "I woke up when that thing hit me on the head. I looked up, and he was just standing there."

"I guess we should just sit here and stare back, don't move," said Beau. "He looks really scared of us. I've never known anyone to be scared of a Labrador. Doesn't he know we are friendly dogs? Check out that cool outfit he is wearing. He looks really nice too," Beau continued, being his typical analytical* self.

Quincy agreed with Beau. "We are in a whole different place. These Maldives people might not be friendly," Quincy lay as still as he could.

Suddenly the boy spoke, "But I am friendly and I have never heard of a Labrador Retriever as you call yourselves. My name is Hassan. I am the son of the Sultan Muhammad of the Huraa Dynasty. Please do not be afraid. The people here in Male Atoll are very friendly and I see you have found one of our most valuable Cowry* that we use for our special ceremonies. I am so sorry I have dropped my flute on your head. Please forgive me," Hassan gave a slight bow and smiled at Beau and Quincy.

"You can understand us," Beau asked.

Both dogs look amazed and astonished! How could this human possibly understand *"Dog Language"*?

"Well of course I can," said Hassan. "I was born with the gift of understanding all animal creatures. This is a gift that some people in my family are born with. However, some animals I meet are not as friendly as you are."

"That is so cool," said Quincy. "We have never known any humans to really understand dog language."

"Cool? No. I am so sorry. Unfortunately, it is most always very warm here," said Hassan.

"I must hurry and get to the Sultan's Castle. We are having a celebration this evening and I must play my flute," Hassan gathered up his flute.

"I was practicing for the celebration when I came upon you two. Would you like to join me? I will have to tether you so the others won't be afraid. You are a large and a new breed of animal here. I assure you though, it will be a fun evening." Hassan put his hands together and begged the dogs to join him.

"I don't see why not," said Beau, "but, we must remember this spot so we will be able to get back to our home again. We just arrived at your land. We kind of... dropped from the sky... I think"

"Let's pile up some rocks to mark the spot and then go with Hassan. I'm famished*," said Quincy.

Quickly, Beau, Quincy, and their new friend Hassan marked the spot with giant rocks. Although the dogs were excited to have dinner with their new friend, they were also very worried because they didn't know how to get home.

They quickly got over their worries and began to enjoy the great adventure.

Off they ran to the castle with Hassan leading the way with his robe fluttering in the wind and his hand on his hat so it would not fall off.

Hassan also held their special shell in the other hand for Beau and Quincy as the dogs did not want to leave it behind.

The Adventures of Beau and Quincy

Chapter 5:
A Royal Bath

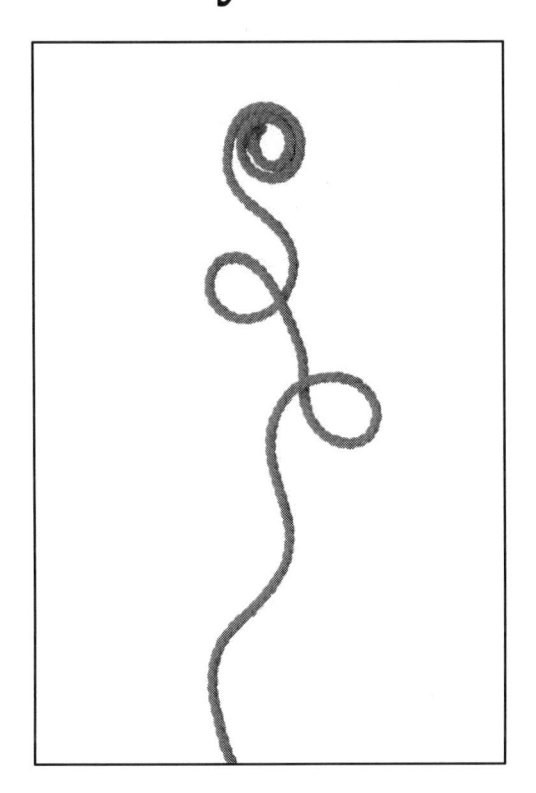

Beau, Quincy, and their new friend Hassan entered through the back entrance of the castle so as to not startle anyone. They rushed to Hassan's chambers.

" Come Beau and Quincy," Hassan said. "I will brush your fur, spray a bit of tonic on you, and tie a golden string around the loop on your… what do you call this?" Hassan pointed to the Quincy's neck Collar.

"That is a collar from our owner. It has our phone number in case we get lost," Quincy explained. "All dogs where we come from must have this."

"Hmmm," Hassan mumbled, "Tonight you will be my guests and you will look most festive and smell as if you have just had a bath. My father, the Sultan, will be so pleased to meet you." Hassan was so excited about getting the dogs ready for dinner that he almost forgot to prepare himself!

Suddenly, in walked a beautiful young teenage looking girl with long dark braided hair who looked similar to Hassan. Hassan gently asked Beau and Quincy to sit. "Good evening Camille," said Hassan, "is the Sultan ready?"

"Not quite," said Camille, "but I came to get the young Sultan ready as I know you are always late. Who are your new friends?"

Camille busily helped Hassan fix his robe, change his sandals, comb his hair, clean the sand off his face, and sprayed tonic on him as well. She also added some shiny jewels made of gold and shells to his clothes. After Camille finished dressing him, he looked just like a Sultan.

Hassan replied, "These handsome creatures are my new friends Beau and Quincy. They are guests visiting from a far away place called Florida. They are very friendly and don't you worry sister, I will keep them tethered*," Hassan pointed to two golden strings.

" Well, ok, but remember what happened the last time you brought animal friends to the celebration," his sister said, looking worried.

"Yes, yes," he replied. "These are a calm species, not like those wild monkeys I brought at that time. I had no idea they would start climbing the walls and screeching when they heard the music!" Hassan sounded truly apologetic.

" Just keep the animals tethered and quiet and everything will be fine," whispered Camille as she whisked* out the door, "and hurry up brother!"

"O.K., we are ready. Oh, I forgot one thing, your shell. I have placed it in this silk bag to tie it on your neck so you do not lose it. I know how important it is to you Labradors," exclaimed Hassan as he tied a sturdy knot around the silk cloth bag onto Quincy's collar. "Hmmm, perfect. This should do fine. You both look exquisite, and you smell great too," he exclaimed.

"And so do you!" Beau and Quincy said in return.

Chapter 6:
The Gift

A minute later, they were out the chamber door and on the way to the celebration. They were with Hassan standing tall and proud, having never experienced such an elegant affair. As they entered the giant ballroom, all eyes of the party were upon them.

Quincy whispered to Beau, "Are my ears twitching? Can you see?"

" No, they are fine. You are just nervous. Just think about all the delicious food smells," Beau whispered back.

Quincy took a deep sniff and said, "Yummm! That is the most delicious smell... kind of like Mom's Chinese food, but with a twist," whispered Quincy and he took a deep sniff again.

" Let's hope we get to try some!" Beau had to stop himself from drooling!

" Don't worry boys, you will be served a big Bowl. Be patient!" Hassan whispered out of the corner of his mouth. "We must sit first and join my Father and Mother and family."

The three walked proudly to the long feast table right towards the head of the table and sat next to the Sultan himself. The feast had already begun as the food was already on the table and the guests were enjoying the variety of colorful exotic* cuisine.

"Good evening my son," said Sultan Muhammad. "Thank you for joining my birthday celebration, my dear boy. These creatures must be my gifts for the evening. They are fabulous. So handsome and well trained. What are they called?" The Sultan asked.

" They are called Beau and Quincy and their species is in the canine family and they are Labrador Retrievers. These are my special guests for the evening, here to celebrate your birthday, though, not gifts. They are from another land. They have come to show you their respect. They have, however, brought you a celebration gift!" Hassan proclaimed. He knew

Beau and Quincy already had a family and couldn't belong to the Sultan.

" Oh, wonderful, I do love gifts! Let us see this treasure!" The Sultan was truly excited.

Hassan pulled the silk satchel from Beau's neck and presented the Cowry*. "the most beautiful and rare."

Beau and Quincy swallowed hard as they watched their chances of getting home disappear from their reach.

Hassan whispered to them, "Sorry, I'll get it back."

" Oh Hassan, you are always full of surprises! The Sultan held the shell over his head up high and exclaimed at the top of his voice as the room fell quiet,

"The best gift of my birthday! Happy 1775 and Cheers to all! Eat and celebrate!"

The Sultan rubbed the shell as if it were a giant diamond. He was truly honored and truly loved it.

Chapter 7:
1775

"We have got to make a plan," said Beau. "We need Mom's shell back!"

"Can't we just find another?" asked Quincy.

"Boys, easier said than done. That is a rare one and not so easy to find," whispered Hassan sadly. "I was just so scared when he thought you were the gift. I had to come up with something to distract him. Here is your dinner, eat up and we will make a plan."

Beau and Quincy gobbled down their bowls of spicy rice and vegetables: the local Maldives cuisine.

" Quincy?" Beau whispered in between bites. "Why did he say it was 1775?"

Quincy replied, "I heard that too. Strange… right? We will have to ask Hassan about that after dinner."

The festivities lasted long into the night, with singing, dancing, and many exotic foods. Beau and Quincy had never had so much fun in their lives. Finally, the big performance was announced to conclude the evening!

"Here he goes, Quincy! Hassan is going to play that flute!" Beau shouted with excitement, but to the rest of the crowd, it came out as a howl!

"Woo Woo," Beau joined in with another howl.

All the audience was cheering. Then suddenly, they fell silent as Hassan lifted the flute to his lips.

Hassan's playing was magical: Each tone was clear and crisp. It was like nothing they had heard before. They had heard cousins playing piano, saxophone, violin, and guitar but never a flute.

"It is like we are in a dream Quincy," Beau stated. "The tone is perfect and makes me feel like I am floating."

"Hold on brother," Quincy said. "Don't let it carry you away. I'm going to need you to get back home. If we are actually in 1775, we have a long way to go to 2023," whispered Quincy as the music began to put him in a trance.

"Enjoy the moment, Quincy, we will figure it out! This is just the most amazing music I have ever heard. Quiet," Beau whispered.

As soon as Hassan had completed his musical piece, the crowd roared with cheers. The Sultan walked to his son and kissed his forehead.

"Congratulations, my son, you have done well," The Sultan announced. "The celebration is over and the evening has been a success. Thank you guests for sharing my birthday festivities. Here is to another successful year, here...here!" as the Sultan raised his golden chalice*!

Quincy eyed the shell at The Sultan's spot at the table. He thought to himself now might be his only chance to grab it. He was worried that without the shell, they would never get home.

Did he really think that Shell was going to get him home? Hmmmm, it got us here.

While Hassan was busy being congratulated and not holding the golden tether, Quincy slowly walked over to the table, reached up, ahhhh, and grabbed it. He walked over to Beau and slipped it into the silk satchel.

"Come Beau. We must get out of here now or we might never get home," Quincy whispered into his ear.

"But don't you trust Hassan? He said he would get it back," Beau questioned Quincy, feeling that he had betrayed their new friend.

"I just want to get home. I love this adventure, but really, I worry about Mom and Dad," Quincy blurted out.

"Well, I feel we are here for a reason," Beau said, "and we just haven't figured out the reason yet."

"Fine," Quincy said stubbornly and sat there waiting for Hassan with Beau.

Hassan returned with his father, The Sultan.

"Where is the cowry?" asked the Sultan.

"Beau here is protecting it in the silk satchel," Hassan pointed to the satchel on Beau's neck. "This way, none of the guests could have accidentally walked out with it," explained Hassan.

"You are a very smart young man, and "*Sultan to Be*" Hassan. Take your animals and run and play and thank you for that beautiful flute playing this evening. Your hours of practicing and lessons have made you the best on our island," the Sultan hugged his son and pardoned himself as he departed.

"Phew," said Hassan. "Nice play on the cowry, Quincy and Beau!"

"You're not angry with us?" Quincy asked.

"Absolutely not! I had no idea how I was ever going to get that shell back. Now Father just thinks that I am keeping it safely for him in my chambers. Hopefully, he will not be asking for it anytime soon," Hassan excitedly blurted out as he led the dogs as they all ran to his chambers.

"When we get back to my chambers," Hassan wheezed out of breath, "we will make a plan for you to get home with the cowry. You do know how to get home, don't you?"

Chapter 8:
No Computers

There was the dilemma: how to get home? When they got back to Hassan's Chambers, Hassan fell sound asleep from the excitement of the day, as an 11yr old boy would, but Beau and Quincy lay wide awake thinking of their return to Florida to Mom and Dad.

"So, if we came through the computer, can't we just go back through a computer?" asked Quincy.

"There's only one problem, Quincy. It's 1775 and there are no computers. They haven't been invented yet. I heard Dad saying once that they weren't even invented till 1822 by a guy named Charles Babbage. But what good would that do us? We need to go to 2023," explained Beau.

"Hmmm, okay, I say we take the shell, hold it in our mouths the exact same way we did before and sit in the very same spot we marked on the beach and see what happens," Quincy suggested.

"Good idea. Let's try it tomorrow," Beau said sleepily.

"How about now! I mean, we run down to the beach now!" Quincy was so excited he couldn't hold back.

"Quincy, I need some sleep, my bones are a little older than yours and they are tired. Tomorrow, okay?"

Beau stretched, rolled over, stretched again, curled up onto a nice big cushion Hassan had set out and was asleep almost instantly.

Quincy began to pace. "How could they all sleep at a time like this." He found a gold ball of string and began tossing it around and when it landed in a basket, he thought to himself, hmmmm, that looks fun.

Soon, Quincy had chewed the corner of the basket and left shreds of dried grass all over the room.

"Now I'm tired." Off to sleep, he went on his own big comfortable cushion from Hassan.

Chapter 9:
Plan to Get Home

Beau awoke first the next morning to see Quincy's mess. "Quincy, get up you trouble maker. What were you thinking?" Beau stared at the shredded corner of the basket. You know Mom gets angry when we do that," Beau grumbled.

Hassan heard the commotion and awoke.

"What's up, boys?" Hassan said, rubbing his eyes and looking around the room. "Oh, that old basket, don't worry, I can mend it later. I learned how to weave baskets when I was little. Now let's figure out our plan!"

Quincy explained his plan and Hassan agreed to give it a try. He too agreed that he had never heard of a computer. He had something called an abacus* that helped to count numbers, but it did not have pictures on it.

"Let's go," said Quincy.

"I must join The Sultan for morning meal," said Hassan.

"Sounds great to me. I am starving and the food here in the Maldives is delicious!" Anyway, we will need a lot of energy for today," reasoned Beau.

"Agreed," they all said together.

Hassan tethered the dogs and off to breakfast they went. Bowls of more delicious rice and vegetable and fruits were set in front of them.

"So what are your plans today?" asked the Sultan.

"We have decided to go to the beach and search for more valuable cowry," explained Hassan.

"Well, let me keep watch of the other one while you are gone, so it remains safe," insisted The Sultan.

"Oh no Father see here, it is very safe tethered to the dog's neck," Hassan assured his father.

"I insist, Hassan," the Sultan said sternly. "I will store it in my gold chest next to my bed."

"Yes sir, father. We will return before sunset," Hassan said, defeated.

When the three finished eating, out the back door of the castle they went, but with no cowry.

"How is this plan going to work," Quincy almost cried.

"Well," said Hassan, "let's try to be positive. We are going to cowry hunt, or shell hunt as you call it. After, we can go to the market and trade what we have found for one that looks similar to yours. Then, we secretly switch it out with your shell that my father is guarding. Is that a great plan or what?" Hassan was always positive.

"Great idea!" Beau said enthusiastically, trying to cheer Quincy up. "It could work and it just adds one more day."

Chapter 10:
Cowry Hunt

Hassan, Beau, and Quincy spent all day on the beach digging and in the surf feeling around for the best cowries.

In the Maldives in 1775, shells were like money. The three filled the basket, the one with the chewed corner, with the most beautiful shiny shells of all types, but none as big and as perfect as theirs.

They did however have a successful day and had fun frolicking in the waves.

"I just love digging on the beach!" Quincy yelled at the top of his voice. "Hey, look at this one, it's awesome, white and shiny and big!"

"That one is worth a lot," said Hassan. "Good find!"

Beau was sloshing at the edge of the water, "Check this out, it's long and dark colored."

"That's a great one too, Beau! Keep it up, guys. We will have great luck at the market!"

Hassan was thinking positively and hopeful that they would find enough shells to then trade for a shell similar to one that looked like theirs. Beau and Quincy's shell was a rare beauty.

After hours of work and a full basket, they called it quits.

Hassan yelled, "Come on boys. Jump in the water and rinse off. The sand can be very sticky."

The water felt deliciously soothing to their tired bodies as they thoroughly rinsed the sand from their fur.

"Are you ready for the market?" asked Hassan.

Beau and Quincy responded, "Ruff, his time."

Hassan let out a giant bellowing laugh, "Hahaha."

Chapter 11:
The Market Crowd

The three dried off and Hassan put the golden tethers on the dogs and they went off to the market. It was a short walk, but wow, what a crowd they saw.

"I sure am glad you tethered us, Hassan. I think we would have gotten lost," said Quincy.

"Or stolen," said Hassan. "I'm going to lead you to the shell section of the market. Just stay very close to me. If someone looks mean, just show them little teeth with a growl," Hassan was not kidding.

"Quincy, don't dawdle, keep up," said Beau. As they weaved their way through the crowd, all the people looked at them wide-eyed and scared.

"We have arrived," announced Hassan. "Follow me into this hut and keep very quiet while I speak."

"Hello Matti, I am Hassan, the son of The Sultan, remember me."

"Ah, yes Hassan," Matti said as he bowed to Hassan. "What can I do for you, young Sultan?"

"We are looking for a larger shell as a gift for my father. We have collected many cowries to pay you with and many are very valuable. Do you have any of the very large ones that we may be searching out?" Hassan asked politely but with royalty in his tone.

"Let me have a look, Hassan, at my full collection. I will return in a moment," Matti disappeared behind a curtain to a back room. He returned in a moment with a basket containing some large shells.

"Let us have a look," said Hassan.

Hassan explained to Beau and Quincy that it was considered bad luck to touch another person's cowry. As he and Beau and Quincy looked into the basket without touching, they were amazed at the number of beautiful shells.

"They look quite nice," said Hassan, "Do you have any with brown swirls in them?"

"Oh Hassan," said Matti, "those types are very valuable indeed. I will go look at my collection again." Matti disappeared behind his curtain again.

Matti returned back in a minute with one more shell.

"Now that is just what we are looking for," Hassan whispered to the dogs.

Hassan now needed to make a deal.

"Our collection is quite valuable. Would you be willing to take our collection in exchange for your one larger cowry?" Hassan asked Matti.

Matti smiled and nodded in agreement.

"Can you please wrap it up in brown silk cloth? Thank you very much, Matti. It was wonderful to see you." Hassan hid his excitement as he walked out the door. He had to play it cool, so Matti continued to think he got the better deal.

Chapter 12:
The Necklace

Now that the three friends had obtained their prize, they quickly left the market. Hassan explained that they would head back to the castle and secretly exchange the new cowry for Beau and Quincy's shell that was stored in his father's gold chest.

"Ugh, how will you sneak into your father's room?" Beau asked.

"Well, I thought that maybe, you two could entertain my father while I make the exchange. What do you think?"

Beau and Quincy wondered how they would keep the Sultan's attention while Hassan made the exchange. Fortunately, Hassan had a plan.

Hassan explained how his father, the Sultan, loved to hide things for his son Hassan to find. It was a treasure-hunting game that Hassan often played with his father. His father would usually hide nuts and fruit. Hassan explained that he would ask his father to play the game with Beau and Quincy. Hassan knew that, with Beau and Quincy's long snouts, that they would be able to find the treats easily.

"Oh, this sounds like such fun! Can we eat the treats when we find them?" asked Quincy.

"Of course you can," Hassan giggled.

Upon arriving back at the castle, there seemed to be a ruckus* in the entry hallway. Hassan's sister Camille was running around frantically* looking for something.

"Oh, Hassan, I'm so glad you're back. Our Mother, The Sultana, has misplaced her favorite pearl and diamond necklace. Father and Mother and everyone in the castle have been searching for hours. They are entertaining a neighboring royal family this evening and you know how Mother always wears that necklace. Please help us search," Camille begged her brother.

"Of course we can. My friends Beau and Quincy have the best noses in the castle. We will find her necklace! Come Beau and Quincy! Smell this pashmina* of my Mother's. The scent will help you find the necklace. It must be in her chambers as I saw her wearing it last night at Father's birthday," Hassan explained.

Hassan, Beau and Quincy ran up the curving stairs to The Sultana's chambers. They searched in every drawer, every closet, and under every cushion.

"Ruff, Ruff, Ruff," Quincy began to bark excitedly. "I smell something under the corner of this rug! Help me move it."

Hassan came running to Quincy's bark and lifted the rug. And there it was, the missing necklace!

Everyone in the castle was overjoyed, especially the Sultan and Sultana, Hassan's mother and father.

"Quincy, I would like to give you a reward for finding the necklace," exclaimed the Sultan. "What do you desire?"

Quincy barked and barked, but only Hassan and Beau could understand him. "Oh, thank you, Sultan. I would love to have the cowry back that we gave you for your birthday. I know it is bad to ask for a gift back, but I really need it to get home!"

Hassan interpreted what Quincy had said and the Sultan immediately ran to his room to gather the cowry from his gold chest.

He tied the cowry around Quincy's neck and hugged him and then hugged Beau.

"I know you must leave, but please come back and visit again soon," The Sultan said.

Chapter 13:
The Marked Spot

The people in the castle were brimming with happiness, but also sad that Beau and Quincy were leaving. They all said their farewells and

Beau, Quincy and Hassan headed to the spot on the beach where they first met.

The day was perfectly quiet and peaceful, just like the day they had arrived.

"I have a surprise for you both that I thought might help in your return home," Hassan showed them his flute. "I will play the same song that I was playing when we met!"

"Oh, thank you, Hassan," Beau and Quincy said together.

"So, what do you think? Do you think we just go to the spot and zap? We will be home," wondered Beau out loud.

"I think we hold the shell and run to our spot as fast as we can, and maybe that will work," Quincy said.

"And as you run, I will play that same song on my flute," Hassan exclaimed. "I think it will work!"

It was decided. They would follow that plan. In the distance down the beach, they could see their marked spot on the beach where they had arrived. Suddenly, the dogs were sad.

They had to say goodbye to their new friend. Hassan hugged them both and kissed them each on the nose.

"Please come back and visit again soon. I will never forget you," Hassan had tears in his eyes.

"We promise we will try to come back someday," said Beau and Quincy as they both kissed Hassan's cheek.

Beau and Quincy gathered their courage and Hassan began to play his flute and they took off running.

As the spot got closer, the air felt warmer, and suddenly their feet lifted off the ground, and everything around them went dark.

Chapter 14:
Home Sweet Home

Beau and Quincy opened their eyes and they found themselves comfortably laying on the kitchen floor by Mom's computer as they had never left. Mom then walked into the kitchen, apologizing to them for being on the phone with Chase (their cousin and Mom's oldest grandson), who had just finished his last exam of law school.

"What is my shell doing on the floor here, boys? Did you steal it, Quincy," she asked while laughing and gently returning it to the living room table.

Beau and Quincy looked at each other in wonder. They just could not believe what had happened to them.

In Florida, no time had passed. They wondered if their three-day adventure was a dream.

The End

Vocabulary

The Sultan and the Seashell

<u>Words and Meaning</u>

- **Monotonous:** *Extremely boring or unexciting*

- **Bauble:** *A small showy trinket or decoration*

- **Regal:** *Fit for a monarch or king. Dignified*

- **Antics:** *Amusing behavior*

- **Cowry:** *A large shiny domed shell found in the indo-pacific*

- **Famished:** *Very hungry*

- **Tethered:** *Tied*

- **Whisked:** *To move suddenly*

- **Exotic:** *Different, strange or unusual*

- **Chalice***: A large cup or goblet*

- **Abacus:** *A calculation tool with beads and rods*

- **Frantically:** *Hurried, distraught*

- **Pashmina:** *Fine quality material scarf made of goat's wool*

The Adventures of Beau and Quincy

Look for Beau and Quincy's next adventure in

Book 2

"Monkeys and Waves"

Made in the USA
Columbia, SC
19 January 2024

4642581a-74b2-427e-a035-163869a23e77R03